King & Kayla

and the Case of the
Cat Hunt

Written by
Dori Hillestad Butler

Illustrated by
Nancy Meyers

PEACHTREE

ATLANTA

For my neighbor, Dave. And his cat, Blue

—D. H. B.

For Cannon, who has so many awesome ideas

for more King & Kayla adventures!

—N. M.

Published by
PEACHTREE PUBLISHING COMPANY INC.
1700 Chattahoochee Avenue
Atlanta, Georgia 30318-2112
PeachtreeBooks.com

Text © 2023 by Dori Hillestad Butler
Illustrations © 2023 by Nancy Meyers

Edited by Kathy Landwehr
Design and composition by Adela Pons
The illustrations were drawn in pencil with color added digitally.

Printed in September 2022 by Toppan Leefung in China
10 9 8 7 6 5 4 3 2 1 (hardcover)
10 9 8 7 6 5 4 3 2 1 (trade paperback)
First Edition

HC ISBN: 978-1-68263-467-7
PB ISBN: 978-1-68263-468-4

Cataloging-in-Publication Data is available from the Library of Congress.

Contents

Chapter One

A New Friend

Hello!

My name is King. I'm a dog. This is Kayla. She is my human.

And this is Raj. I don't know him. But Kayla does.

"I heard you're a detective," Raj says to Kayla.

"We are both detectives!" I say.

"King, off," Kayla says.

"Sorry," I say.

"Can you help me find my missing
    cat?" Raj asks.

"I'll try," Kayla says.
"What's his name?"

"Blue," Raj says. "But he's not really blue.
He's gray with dark stripes. And he has
yellow eyes."

Hey! I know a cat like that.
But his name isn't Blue.
It's Cat with No Name!

"When did you last see Blue?" Kayla asks.

"Yesterday morning," Raj says. "He ate his breakfast. But last night's dinner is still in his bowl."

WHAT? Blue skipped dinner?

"He never goes outside, so he's got to be somewhere in the house," Raj says. "But we've looked everywhere."

"Except where he is," Kayla says. "Come on. Let's go to your house."

"Wait for me," I say. Because wherever Kayla goes, I go!

Chapter Two

Raj's House

"Come in," Raj says.

Sniff...sniff... I smell cat. But I don't think that cat is here.

"Where does Blue like to hang out?" Kayla asks.

"I'll show you his favorite hiding places," Raj says.

We look behind
the sofa. No Blue.

We look under Raj's dad's bed.
No Blue.

We even look up at the boards in the
basement ceiling.

"That's where we found
him the last time he went
missing," Raj says.

"How did he get up there?"
Kayla asks.

Raj shrugs.

"Were all your doors and windows closed yesterday?" Kayla asks.

"The door to the roof deck may have been open," Raj says. "But he couldn't have jumped off the roof."

"Can I see your roof deck?" Kayla asks.

"Sure," Raj says.

We go up some stairs.
Then up more stairs.
Then out a door.

Sniff...sniff...

I smell birds...flowers...squirrels...

And if I try hard, I also smell cat!

We look under the chairs. No Blue.

We look behind a plant. No Blue.

We go to the railing.

Hey, we can see the whole world from up here.

Including the dog park! I LOVE the dog park. It's my favorite place!

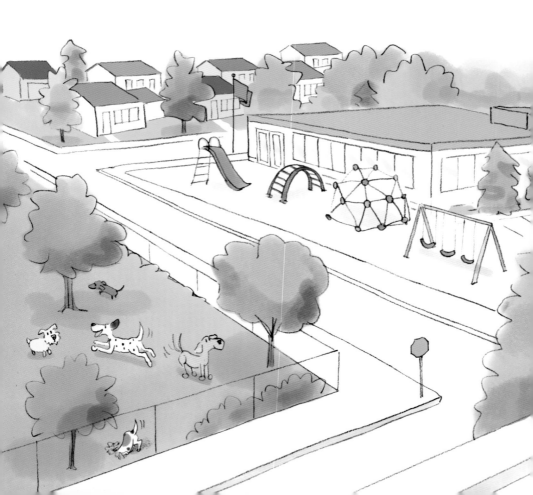

"You're right, Raj," Kayla says. "Blue couldn't have jumped down from here."

"What should we do now?" Raj asks. "Talk to my neighbors or put up lost cat signs?"

"Both!" Kayla says.

Chapter Three

A Sneezy Neighbor

Raj and Kayla make a sign on the computer. Then they print eleventy two copies of it.

The cat on their signs looks a lot like Cat with No Name!

I wonder if Cat with No Name has a name. Could his name be Blue?

We put up the signs around Raj's neighborhood.

I keep watch for Cat with No Name.

We talk to Raj's neighbors.

"Have you seen this cat?" Kayla asks.

"No," a woman says.

"Have you seen this cat?" Raj asks
a man with a red nose.

"Ah…AH…AHHHH CHOOOOOOO!!!!!"
the man says. "Sorry. I'm so allergic
to cats that even a picture of one
makes me sneeze."

"Really?" Raj asks.

"Is that even possible?" Kayla asks.

The man sneezes again. "I haven't seen your cat," he tells Raj.

We go back to Raj's house.

Kayla grabs a notebook and pencil. "Let's make a list of everything we *know* about this case," she says.

1. Raj hasn't seen Blue since yesterday morning.

2. Blue didn't eat his dinner last night.

3. The door to the roof deck may have
   been open. All the other doors and
   windows were closed.

If I could write, I would add this to
Kayla's list of things we *know*:

"Now let's make a list of what we *don't know* about this case," Kayla says.

1. Did Blue get out of Raj's house?

2. If so, how?

3. Why hasn't he come home?

If I could write, I would add this to Kayla's list of things we *don't know*:

"Now we need a *plan*," Kayla says.

I have a *plan*:

Find Cat with No Name.

Chapter Four

What Dog Across the Street?

I run to the door. "Let's go find Cat with No Name!" I say.

"No, King. We're not going home yet," Kayla says. "Not until we find Blue."

"He's not here," I tell Kayla. "We need to find Cat with No Name. He could be Raj's missing cat!"

Kayla doesn't understand a word I'm saying.

I go to the window. "WHERE ARE
YOU, CAT WITH NO NAME?" I call.

"What are you barking at, King?"
Kayla asks.

"I think he sees the dog across the
street," Raj says.

"What dog across the street?" I ask.

Oh. That dog across the street.

"Hello there," that dog calls.
"I'm Goldy. What's your name?"

"King," I say. My tail wags
all by itself.

"Are you looking for a cat?"
Goldy asks.

"Yes! He's gray with dark
stripes and—"

Kayla drags me away from the window. "Stop barking and lie down," she says.

I lie down.

But I really, really, really want to get up!

"There's a cat in your upstairs
window," Goldy says.

There is?

I've GOT to go check that out.
I'm sure Kayla won't mind...

Chapter Five

Rescued by a Dog

There's no cat up here.

"Not that window," Goldy says. "*That* window." She points with her nose.

There is no other window. There's just a wall.

Hey! I hear something on the other side of that wall. It sounds like scratching.

"Cat with No Name? Blue? Is that
   you?" I ask.

"GET ME OUT OF HERE!" the
   cat yells.

"Where are you?" I ask.

"Next door!" he says.

How did he get next door?

Wait. I think I know...

"King, come!" Kayla calls. She claps her hands.

"No. You come. I think I've solved our case," I say. I charge up the stairs to the roof deck.

I jump over the wall.

"NO, KING!" Kayla yells.

I paw at the door.

Finally someone opens it. It's the man
with the red nose!

"Excuse me!" I say.

Sniff...sniff...

Where is that cat?

Aha! He's in there!

The man opens the door and a cat
leaps into Raj's arms.

"Hey, you're not Cat with No Name!"
I say.

"No. I'm Blue," the cat says.

"Ah...CHOOOO!!!!" the man says.

"You shouldn't barge into people's houses, King," Kayla says. "But I'm glad you found Blue."

"Please take the cat away," the man says.

"Sorry he got out," Raj says. "We'll make sure the door to our roof deck stays closed from now on."

"Rescued by a dog? Hmph!" Blue snorts.

On our way home, Kayla and I stop to meet Goldy in person.

And look! Goldy's people have hamburgers. I LOVE hamburgers. They're my favorite food!

GULP!

"Mmm! Thank you," I say.

The End

Oh, boy! I LOVE books.
They're my favorite things!

"...a great introduction to mysteries, gathering facts, and analytical thinking for an unusually young set."
—*Booklist*

"A perfect option for newly independent readers ready to start transitioning from easy readers to beginning chapter books."—*School Library Journal*

"Readers will connect with this charmingly misunderstood pup (along with his exasperated howls, excited tail wagging, and sheepish grins)." —*Kirkus Reviews*